LAND BEAST

KATE WYER

illustrations by KATIE FEILD

CEROS PRESS
Baltimore, MD

Copyright © 2015
ISBN: 978-0-692-53009-2
Cover and book design by Katie Feild

Ceros Press
Baltimore, MD

landbeastnovel.org

All proceeds go to anti-poaching charities.

For all inquiries, including requests for review materials, please contact
landbeastnovel@gmail.com

to the beast
who inspired
this story

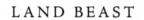

LAND BEAST

PART ONE

There are great kelp bladders, air mouthed into their growth, fed into them. The process of lifting near rootless: sea constant against each hollow knuckle: falling, unfalling.

I have no built-in buoy. I collapse into the undrinkable.

But mostly, I remember the river. My head rooted under that water, pulling against anything that wanted to lift. The plants thin green and mucus-rich in my teeth.

Arms, off. Legs, off. No, that's not true. Just the horn and some skull.

My breath collapses under sedation. A matter of giving away, of no longer resisting. Heaviness from needled sleep.

I would like to continue.

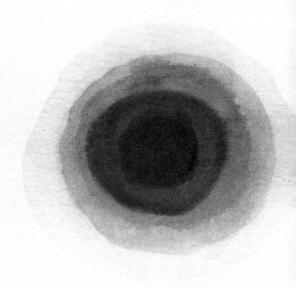

On my side in the dust, my one sky-turned eye sees a brass handle on the diminished moon. I imagine opening that door and seeing a blacker circle there against the black. The moon's gravity shaves away its edges into dust, a constant powder. My vision thick with it, granular.

My eyelashes have been praised. The interior of my ears as well, their deep cones and feathered hair.

The terror-panic of my eyes closing, of feeling the lashes against the rims, of fighting that. I kept my legs moving even when my legs could not feel ground.

I have a daughter.

I imagine her cracked mouth, her dry throat. I imagine her hunger and collapse. I see the way her thin body looked when alone.

I am a land beast and in this story I am in the sea. A creature of simple needs. Mud, protection, grass. The hard roaring of males. I do not struggle against this.

I carried my daughter for sixteen months and my body could not shut off the awareness of her heaviness. I found myself counting sunrises to her birth.

The sea rose and carried me, my two ton body, my rough self. My dried mud toes and caked mud tongue. I woke up, my equilibrium lost. I could not right myself.

It is hard to keep circling around the thing that happened and not say it. But it is also hard to say it. So, I circle some more until it tells itself. I can trust that it will.

I had heard the engines for days, and then the helicopter. Their violence was no secret. My violence was no secret either. I could not ask to be spared. And yet, why not? It's true I have no other predators. It's true I am a killer. But what of the violence of place?

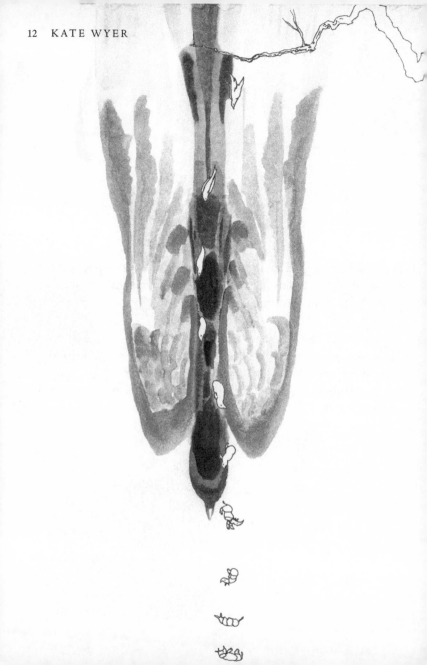

Shorn. Sheared. Not severed, severed would be a limb. I cannot see the way I used to, with all this open space between my eyes. My eyes do not know their sides anymore, right, left: they search the middle. My mind still tries to rope them together in the united way they saw before.

In the dream there, the forced dream of sedation, there was a brass-handled moon. I opened the door and stepped through to the sea.

I could smell gasoline on the men.

Like the boys in the village who hit the sides of metal drums, the sound signaling emptiness, the gas leaping out in drops, arching into the dust, pulling into spheres before sinking.

Like the way a bird folds its wings into its body as it dives from a branch, no fear in the dropping. They know they can stop and lift. Their minds plummet in a controlled way. The birds find what they need: a grub, a song, a mate. Or, they don't. It's the same, though, the falling.

I am a land beast. I am not meant to drop, not into a dark circle, or into the void of falling. I drop only when forced to shut down. When my legs give out.

I am meant to walk footpaths, the same footpaths my mother walked. Her flat feet in that fine dust, the dust of families on their way to water, to shelter. We walk this way. We are easy to track on footpaths.

We heard them from the air. We knew they were coming. We could smell them. We knew that there would be nowhere without them. Men want to believe there is power in our horns. And there is, there is the power they give them. We are full of the life that makes each cell push another out of the way, build and build until they push off the body. We are full of the life needed to make horns.

We ran like the grasslands were on fire.

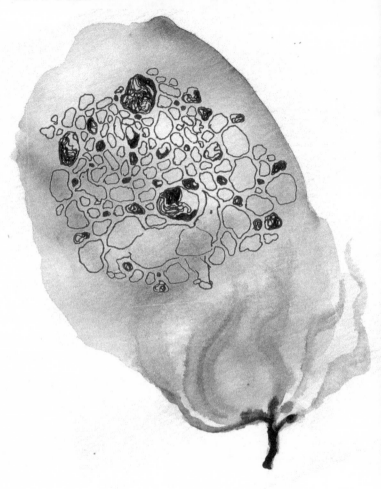

How did I know what the sea was, let alone know how to dream of it? I had never seen it. The water I knew was near stagnant, it had no motion unless others waded in, pushed their bodies into its warmth. How did I know saltwater? The runoff of eyes.

But those small dark marks under eyes know no motion except down.

I knew a river once, when it was still difficult to walk, my legs uncramping and building muscle. A baby of three-hundred pounds. That water against my face was the first and only real coolness I've known. I closed my eyes to it because the water hurt to look through. I tried to see where the water was coming from and what it was made of. I put my head in too deeply and my ears filled up and still I kept pushing down. My mother stood beside me, allowing me this mistake. It was easy to forget to breathe when I hadn't been out of the womb long. But the coolness running over my eyes woke me to my now separateness. I came back up to air.

I tried to shake the water out of my ears. What had been weightless was now pressure that needed release.

What can possibly prepare the body for a chainsaw.

There are other horned beasts. Buffalo, cows, deer, ox. Men use those horns for knife handles and other things. Dogs chew on them for the marrow. The horns clean the dogs' teeth. Those other horned beasts are killed for their meat and the antlers are secondary. Just another useful thing on the carcass.

My body served no other purpose to the hunter.

I've heard of another creature. A creature called a unicorn. One horn. Like me as I was, before.

At the water hole with my daughter, I saw her flip water off her tiny nub, tossing her head back to see the water catch light, bright in its falling.

Can I not talk without mentioning her?

Here it is again, without her:

At the water hole.

That is the story without her.

We all gathered together at dusk, pulled our bodies from the mud and took slow walks around the perimeter, using our feet to crush tall grass. We had to crush it to our mouths' height.

Sometimes wild dogs would stand at the far edges of our circle and bark at us. They would lower their chests to the ground between their front legs and bark and then spring up, pawing the space between us. The young would startle at their sounds. But they witnessed the adults ignoring the dogs, and they learned to ignore. Even the dogs' smell no longer surprised their noses.

We could smell cooking fires in the distance. We could smell bodies in the fires.

Every night after eating I returned to a place under a tree with low branches and enjoyed the coolness of the dust. Life meant a way to keep cool in the sun, a place to eat grass and place to rest. Solitary, mostly.

I was airlifted, but I only know this because I was told. I have the slightest memory of flight, but the memory must be false. Something I created to not lose out. I am a land beast, remember. I am heavy.

I met her father the usual way. He was in a fight and he won. I was five and he was fifteen. I did not run away from him. I did not fear him. I had heard his noise for a few weeks and waited. His smell was not unpleasant.

There were others before me that met the horn-takers. I came upon two of them in the summer. Their bodies had been dead for days and I had not recognized their smell. I knew the female; we came up at the same time. Our mothers wallowed in the same hole and sometimes nuzzled noses in the monsoon season. Everyone was always happiest during the monsoon. There was no need to search out mud. Everything was mud. The greens were always crushed to the right height from the force of the water. There was bleating, honking, celebration.

They call where I am now California. There is no rain here, never.

I was born by a river and never returned to it. I could not find the footpath that brought my mother there. I could not remember the walk I took back from it. I've tried to search my memory for the right pattern of smells and sounds. A particular fruit of a particular tree. The hammering of birds in those trees. Giant cats in green shadows, the scrape of their tongues loud against their paws in cleaning.

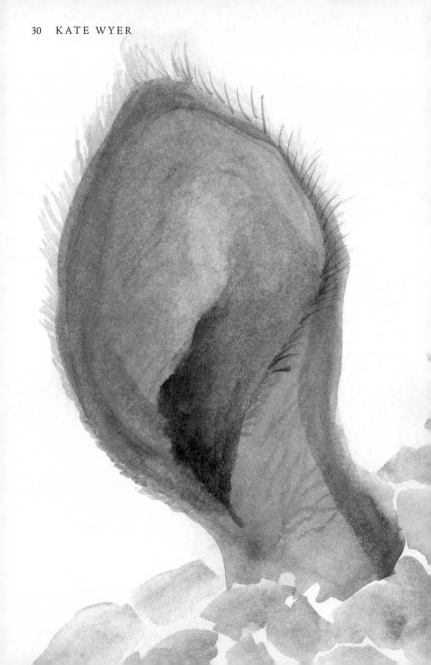

The second one felled was a male I had never seen before. A wanderer from another range, a distant one. His ears held a slightly different cone shape. These two, the male and female, fell together, became hornless. The ground around them had dried once into black dust and was becoming wet again from their bodies and the animals that found them.

There are six documented ways to kill us. The shotgun makes it easy, is used most often. What happened to me was not one of the six. Also, I did not die.

When I used the word "we" when I said "We knew they would be coming" I was talking about my daughter and myself. We were the we. I tried to hide my fear but she knew. She could taste it in my milk. She didn't even know which questions to ask. She knew fear but not death.

Like the butcher who buys grassland for cow pastures. Every day he foresees death in the field. But do the cows know he is coming?

My nose deep in mustard greens, the oils burning the rims and outside edges. The taste a drug, a fire in the throat and tongue. We can smell the fields from miles away and come like vultures to a carcass. And we make those fields carcasses, we clean the bones of the rows, pull the plants up by the roots, send the dirt in showers; our feet high-stepping, as high as they can, in the satisfaction and pleasure.

She had a pot and a pan and she was hitting it to make noise. She wanted to frighten me away from her greens. I was not frightened. I did not move my mouth away from the greens. She came closer, then closer, hitting harder and harder on the metal pot. The sound like a tiny bloodsucker in my ear. The bite unfelt. She smelled like a human, like hunger. Thin skin. She smelled like a rootless scrounger. Go away, I thought. Allow me the claim of this field. This marshland you've filled with rows. She continued her banging. Her pot might bring guns, I thought. The sound might signal guns to come. I lifted her and then she fell. I was only four years old.

I had a belly full of greens and felt sleep coming. I looked for a tree with low branches under which to sink. The blood already drying. It felt like mud, like attenuated mud. It felt like protection. The sun would soon rise and I needed shadow. The oil from the greens so strong in my gut. I was drunk, like the birds that eat fermented berries, those berries at the end of the season that have hung too long on the branch, turned into a mild poison, a pleasant one; those birds that fall over and swoon, sleep deep as death.

Solitary, I washed the blood away. Submerged my horn, closed my nose to the warm water, held my breath. It did not matter, the blood. It would not matter to anyone. I would not see anyone, anyway. It was not monsoon season. There were no crashes of us, no herds. I would not feel the white-red call to mate.

They say lumber. I say walk. I say I run faster than you imagine.

This dream of the sea returns nightly. The great kelp tries to give me their arms. They try to find my mouth and fill it with air from their bladders as I travel down. They know they cannot lift me; they cannot roll themselves around me to keep me floating.

I dreamt of the sea before I knew that was its name. Before it was named it was just a body of water that stung my face where my face was open. In the dreams I could feel this, even after my face had healed.

Mynah birds were screaming. I heard them over the chainsaw as I fought forced sleep.

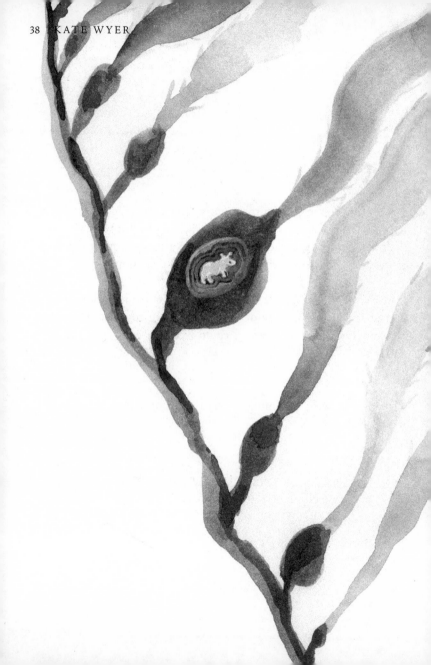

All the seasons cycle through once during pregnancy, then half of the seasons cycle through again before it is over. The baby already knows cold and sparse food; already knows the monsoons and their pleasure; knows the heat and danger of the sun; been with me at the foot of mountains, hung in my belly as I wallowed; knows sprouts; knows the corset of wax around tough plants; knows solitude.

My willful nose remembering her smell.

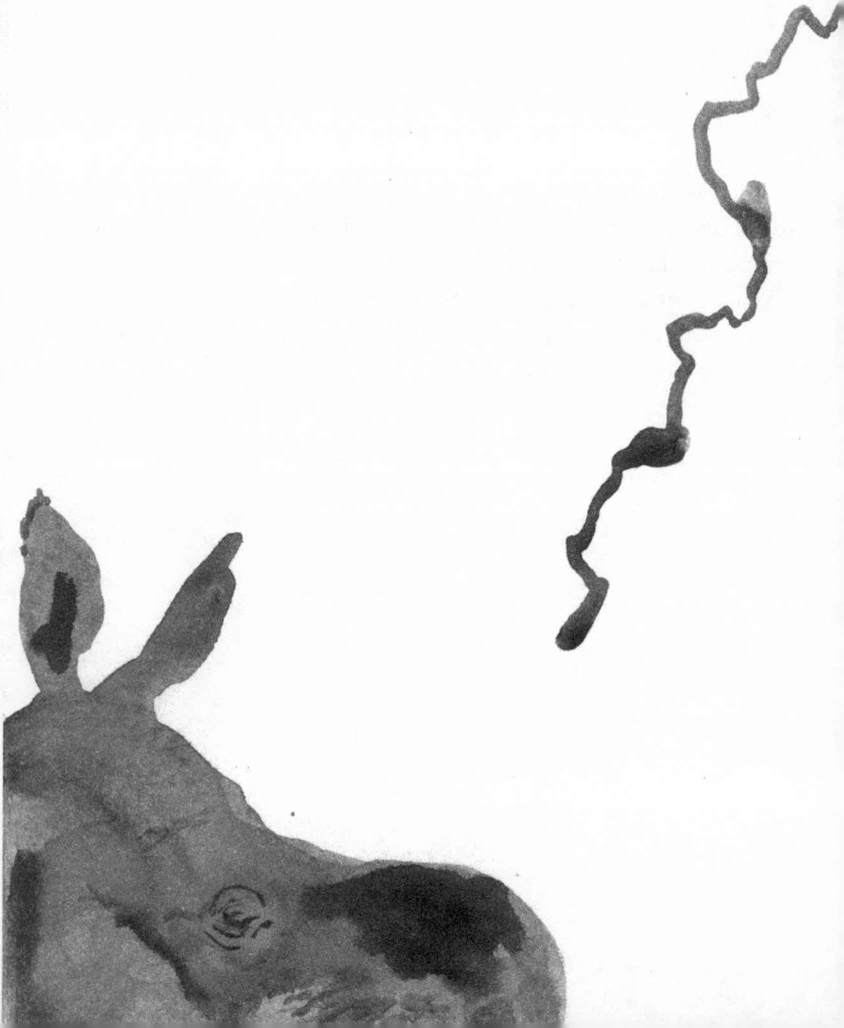

There is a thundering in the horn when there is lighting. The air shakes and vibrates around it; the air fills with static. Blue sparks arc from the horn onto anything: grasses, trees, rocks, hides. The arcing of being to being, sharing the jolt.

My youth: exhausted, willing to push it to zero, to fumes. This is how I ran. Headlong, reckless, shrubs under my feet unfelt, willful blades of feet, birds and rats shooting out of the way of my two-ton body. A riot. A riot. Panting, empty, drinking for ten minutes straight after, feeling heart rate return to normal. A thrashing against the daily routines of waking, eating, wallowing and sleeping.

I am not noble. I am not kind. I was not tender, except. You know, I know you know.

The sadness of grace seen fleetingly. Even through the bandages covering my nose and face, I smelled him. Somewhere there was another. Another was here, after so long in sleep, in flight, in a concrete cage on a straw covered floor, under blankets. The blankets felt like mud, like protection. They allowed quietness. Where was he? Where do they keep him?

The bandages did little to help me. They just made me angry. They made me more aware of what was missing.

Like a till, like a chainsaw, like a bulldozer. Those tools of strength with appetite. My anger.

He greeted me with a snort. I stood there, at the gate to the reserve, full of shame. My cut-down-to-the-skull head. Still I stood, not moving. He came closer. He rubbed the side of his head against the side of mine. The touch a blue arc. A return from the sea.

PART TWO

There is so much field, so much openness. It is possible to forget the fence.

I stand at a distance and watch his shape move across the far edge of the horizon. He is most always there, so mindful of captivity, pressed against the braided wire.

I joined him in his looking those first days. I looked through the patterned light. There was nothing there, meaning: the same trees and grasses, the same stones and dust, as inside the fence.

We are in a canyon and if you lift your eyes to the hills you can see it is open up there too. Singular crows ride the drafts.

I see the crows of home, the land hot with their bird bellies, bellies lifted a few inches from the ground, their claws stirring dust and heat.

Offerings are tossed to them. There are songs to bring songs.

The villagers haul fishing nets and throw them over the murder; the ropes have the heavy murkiness of river water. The crows flatten to the dust, their songs change. Bird by bird they are lifted and brought to the villagers' mouths. A bite to the neck to kill them. The bones are filled with air, an architectonic holiness. The bones were made for what they desired: flight.

Women pluck iridescent black feathers and pile them at their feet. They handle knives and gizzards. They spit chewing tobacco. They make the birds headless and then place the bodies in a pot.

Like rubies in a tumbler. The bodies' edges soften, gleam.

The women turn a plague into a feast.

What about the carrots? Such sweetness. And the melons rolled to us, near splitting with ripeness? Similar to the mangos of home.

What about the absence of fear? The absence of the helicopter and gasoline fumes; the absence of rifles and greed.

The absence of my horn, of the fear it would be taken. The absence of my daughter and the fear for her safety.

To be released from these fears does not mean I am grateful to their takers.

My mind is unfamiliar to me. Like a mother bird who finds a cuckoo egg in her nest. There is no option but to feed the parasite. To feed it as if it were your own.

How I long for a thunderstorm.

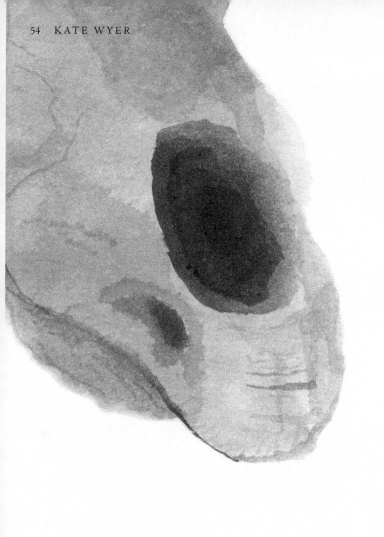

Red beets, golden beets. Their dark greens hold sweetness too. Every week there is a new treasure in the troth near the keepers.

They have women handle me. Before these women, the closest I had been to one was the one I killed. The smell of that kill flares in my nose and makes me pant. How easily my body humiliates me. Shames me.

And how too does my body not allow for grieving. How around the male I am bowed, docile. My mind turns away from loss when I am around him. I feel my milk still building and then realize the heat is not from production, but from the will to produce. Sometimes I feel a slight swaying, a slight unsteadiness—as if returning to land.

I try not to crowd him. It's unnatural to be around him. If we were wild still, wild still unwounded, I would not seek company.

My scabs itch and pull tight. I rub them against a tree until I feel the wetness of blood and know that I've opened them again. I will continue to wound myself until the skin scars and resists me and still I will find ways to open myself.

I watch the outrageous pleasure of the elephant. She sinks her trunk deep into the waterhole and then lifts it to spray her hot back. Her skin is thick like mine. Her child is next to her, leaning against her hind legs.

A locust moves lazy incisors over the hay's chaff. It moves with slow efficiency, rotating the dry stalk, chewing the ripe seed under the husk. It moves with the luxury of a full stomach.

This is how we all move here. Slow, fat. Even the pests are pulled into its safety.

The male, at the far corner alone against the fence, is not slow. Even though he mostly rests his body against the wire, you can see his body is not still. He is not moving and yet he is not still. There is everything under his skin. It is all there.

Once, a woman here ate curry. I smelled it across the field: the coriander, the cumin, the cardamom. I was reminded of a woman at the waterhole, a woman who had walked its perimeter. She was in orange and gold. There was vulgarity in her movement. Something unsettling. I took breaths of her and pulled her into my head. I breathed into the smell and tried to figure out its sourness.

I pulled my feet from their deep place in the mud. My daughter did the same. Even outside of my body she was in me. Every action mirrored, learning and thinking at once.

The woman bent to pull a lotus from the water. She held the stem in both hands, and then ripped the petals from the base. The woman threw petals and then threw the stem with the remaining seed bed. She tried to push the petals into the water with her hands. They were thick and wet; they rolled up under her palms as she tried to push. They were bruised worms: ropes of pale bodies crushed and leaking. They did not float.

My daughter looked to me to see how she should be feeling. I didn't know what to show her, so I remained still and pulled the woman into my nose again. My daughter pulled the woman into her nose too.

She sat near the waterline and rested her hands, face up, on her thighs.

I signaled to my daughter that it is okay to sink again. We allowed the mud to return again to the knees, feet deep in the thick of it. My daughter reached to eat a lotus. She pulled on the thick leaves and sliced through them. The bubble of a root.

This small movement caught the woman's eye. She startled. She stilled her body and watched.

No one moved.

We stayed this way, unmoving, until nerves settled. She lay down, her face near the lip of the water. She clasped her hands together and prayed. She rolled into the shallows and kept her face submerged.

Out, I said to my daughter. Get out of the water, I said.

The woman turned her head to breathe and then returned it underwater. Her orange clothing turned dark brown and the gold lost its glint. Like a coin changing many hands, each leaving its own small corrosion, each hand taking with it some metal.

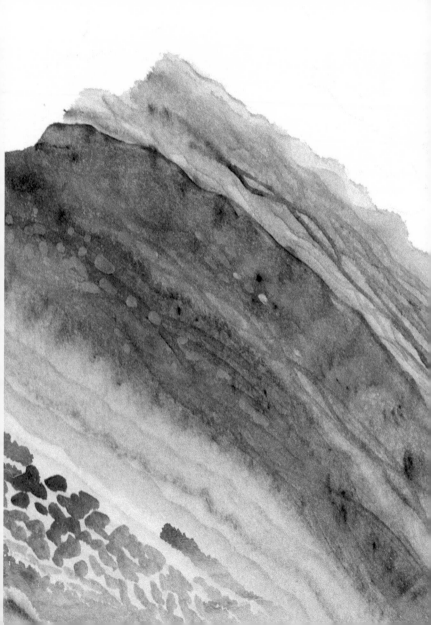

I shake with want.

Let me think again about the airlifting. See my great shadow move across a flat sea. The helicopter's fans move scalped air, carve patterns into the water. I imagine my rolling eyeball looking up at the moon. I am under the belly of the plane, hanging in the darkness, a moon shadow. How much trust they must have put into the cables that held me. How easy it would seem to fray and pull steel fiber from steel fiber. How easy it would seem to lose my body to the sea.

The drop slow, the helicopter losing balance, springing into the sky from sudden weight loss, from the sudden loss of my body suspended in the blackness.

A mind rutted to emptiness, aware only of itself.

Where are the footpaths here? To the trough, to the water, to the trees. The same, really. The same as home.

My body floats within my body: a slight duality, a slight buoyancy, especially something with the mouth. It's like the lips are made aware of the face. They move, prehensile, reaching, wanting to grasp. Like the nerves have their own desires.

I remember water filling my mouth as I ate lilies.

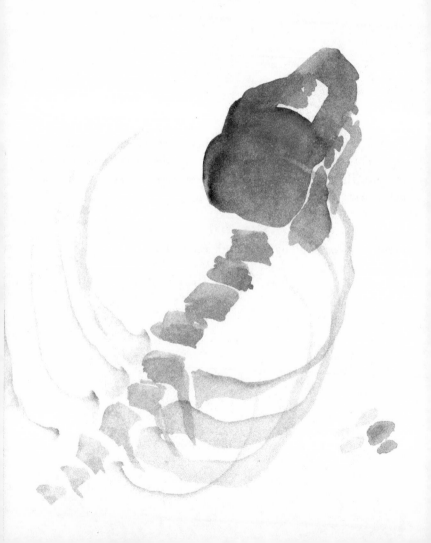

Climb into her chest and look up through the ribs. See where her small neck connected to her skull. See the bone that would have supported her horn. See the toes, like small creatures of their own, like the bones of something smaller. They have a gritty texture from being hollowed out, from being beetle-bored.

The toes like the toes of drought. I place them in my mouth and feel the ridges of her walking this way. Rub them against the roof of the mouth. Spit them out and see them clean and pale. The toes she would have walked away from me on.

I know the dead are pulled into the sky. It is not enough to keep their smell here on the ground.

Ants stop to clean themselves on her. Just another stone to mark on their way. Her body a trail, a collection of hormones.

What happened to the body of the woman I killed? Her body cleaned and burned. Her family wrapped her in linens and brought her body to a fire. They kissed her and burned her. Her death went into the sky too. A ritual of cleanliness.

So many called to do the cleaning.

Except me. If I had stood and gored a wild dog, that would have been cleaning my daughter. If I had stood and crushed beetles, that would have been cleaning. Preventing others, letting only the hardness of my exhaustion fail me.

Pulled away. Dropped into the sea. Watch the shadow fall and the helicopter go up, spin, and readjust after losing two tons. My body taken into the sea. Swallowed.

Once a death goes into the sky, does it return?

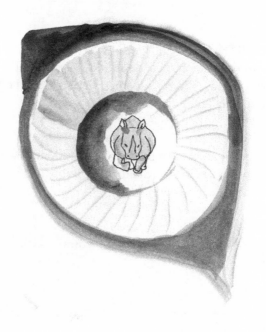

My breathing changes around the male. I want to see his mouth foam for me. I want to see his legs shake for me. This is not power, is it? Both of us must reach toward the other. Does it matter who goes first?

Yes.

While in the sea I felt salt in all the places of my body.

At first I didn't think to think about where my horn was. It wasn't on my body and my body hurt. That was all. Then it was absent and I picked my scabs and they hurt. Then my skin scarred over and I wondered what had happened to the rest of me.

Ground to cure hangovers. Ground to cure impotence. I think about my severed horn and some male drinking it. The deadness of keratin—the absolute powerlessness of a toenail. What a failure of imagination. The shape and strength of my horn will do nothing for you.

Legs clanging in the sea.

The kelp branches are dark against the filtered light. They move like trees in a monsoon. They look like Chitwan trees against the sunrise. That first sun moving, strange and rabid—mist-killing, water-eating, river-hating. There are dark arms against the growing day. There are tunnels in all of us. We carry the same treatment of life, share the same vulnerabilities.

Helicopters are unliving and monsoon loud.

Her body already armored: the plates of her legs, her shoulders, her hips. Her beautiful smooth head.

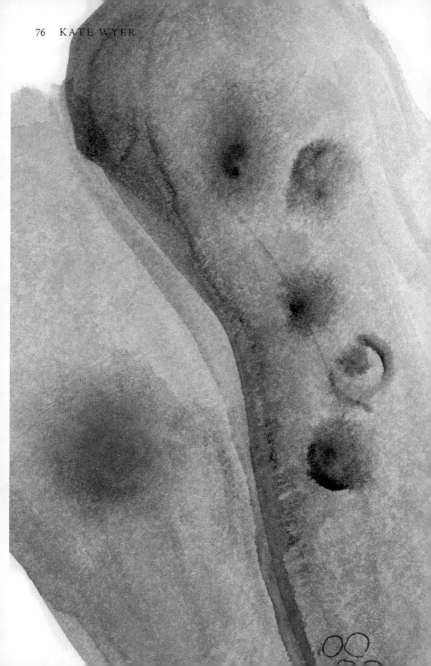

I look for wounds and find them. The silver dollars of bullet scars. I don't know how he lived. I don't know how he kept his horn.

Is it because he is the only one here? The only other like me? If there were two, would I still want this one? This male?

Yes.

I want him to come to me. I don't want to approach his fence-gazing, his ground-gazing, his palpable anger. I want to sheer his ears with my teeth, bite through his upper lip where it becomes his nose. There is nothing tender here. I want to call him with my body and watch his head rise to meet my smell, his thick legs moving toward me, his nose leading.

If I could charge at my rescuers, I would. If I knew the man who had stopped my bleeding and wrapped my wound; if I knew the team that heaved my body into a sling and flew me over the sea; wrestled with the infection of a rusty chainsaw; covered my eyes with bandages until I hallucinated sight and saw my daughter walk away from me, I would charge. My eyes showed me her leaving. I saw her tail swishing away flies, her ears twitching them away. These pests were becoming her normal, the movements to shoo were built into her. From her posture I could tell she wasn't missing me. She was learning to be alone, to be like me, a land beast.

The rescuers could have left my body. They could have shot me through the head to force the life out of me. A kindness, as they say. Like a rabid dog.

We are all this way, I want to say to him. *We are all ground-staring, but there is also a sky. There is also a face to meet your face.*

I watch him—half-black from the water. Black and wet up to his nose, his back still baked clay. The male searches out lily pads and grasses that hold the sweetness of quiet water.

EPILOGUE

There were captured and tamed beasts where I lived before. Home, I mean. Their toe nails were painted, as were their heads. They had riders and bells around their ankles. It was easy to be cruel to them, from our safe, free space. By cruel I mean stand at the edges and show our freedom. With the bells and paint there were also chains.

I wondered about their lives and kept my distance.

They are here, too. Refugees. None of the religion and all of the captivity.

Fringes of colors, bright and open. The people with paint pigments and drums. Before the market of bodies surged. The drumming vibrated in our hollow places too, moving the sound through blood and our own calls for the seasons.

Deities. Possession. Robbery.

Riders in thrones roped to the body. An intimacy in the proximity. In the cast of our eyes and lashes.

An incomprehensible desire for inlays, for spoons. For combs. Make an effigy. Make a pile of them, thousands of them, representing bodies.

Let me smell into sight, into the details of the trail. Let the brain light up into patterns to show me who walked here yesterday. The day before. Their images move through my mind like phantoms, the smell breathes them into tracers of light. The quietness of a mind standing on a footpath and smelling a week's worth of travel.

A burn of a male's scent. The pleasure of a cow's.

Deep in the memory of them, all of them.

INTERVIEW with KATE WYER
by Joseph Scapellato for The Collagist, 2013

Where did Land Beast begin for you and how did it get to here?

"Land Beast" began with an image. I follow a tumblr that posts animal pictures, like blue-tongue skinks or red-legged honeycreepers, some dogs, etc. It's a pleasant way to spend a few minutes. So it was all the more startling when I saw the picture of the female rhino. My mind couldn't process it for a moment—the strangeness of the animal without its distinctive feature and then the brutality of what remained of her face. The caption described her assault, the death of her calf, her rescue and subsequent rehab at a preserve. It also mentioned she was inseparable from the male rhino at the preserve—a very rare thing for solitary animals. She had a wild look in her eye. That look wouldn't leave me alone.

But my way into telling her story is a little less straightforward. I had the first stanza or paragraph—I think calling it a stanza actually works a little better. It was going to be the start of something else, but I wasn't sure what. I knew I liked the sounds that were working within those sentences, but I didn't know what to do with them until I realized they fit into the rhino's experience of being out of her element, of being thrown into something as large and foreign as loss. The idea of collapse became really important to me. Of no longer resisting a fall. I wanted to play with how water supports you and yet it doesn't, much like memory.

Opening myself up this way also permitted me further strangeness, like the moon door and jumping blue arcs of current. Those things allowed me to have the rhino reach for connection.

*As a reader, I'm enchanted by this piece's spell of defamiliarization—
the narrator, who I read as a rhinoceros, allows us to see beauty, terror,
and strangeness in the familiar. I found many passages to be haunting,
especially this one:*

> We heard them from the air. We knew they were coming.
> We could smell them. We knew that there would be
> nowhere without them. Men want to believe there is
> power in our horns. And there is, there is the power they
> give them. We are full of the life that makes each cell push
> another out of the way, build and build until they push
> off the body. We are full of the life needed to make horns.

*My question is, to what extent did this narrator surprise you? (I'd love to
hear about how/when the narrator surprised you the most.)*

Seeing the photo once was enough and I wanted retain the initial
strength of my reaction. After working on the story for a few days
though, I wanted to see pictures of other rhinos to further some
softness in my descriptions. For example, I imagined rhinos to have
huge eyelashes, like a giraffe or a horse-- they don't. But they do
have incredibly soft looking cone-shaped ears. I used The Soul of
the Rhino by Mishra Ottaway to rediscover these details. It's a book
about conservation efforts in Nepal and India. I read the book several
years ago, and had forgotten that rhinos kill people. I realized she was
going to kill someone. That was surprising, but in a terrible way it
felt comfortable. Brutality and brutality. I am able to write violence,
even though I can't stomach it when others do. I am very much a
"close my eyes, block my ears" movie watcher. I realized that her
violence would be fed by the larger violence of habitat loss, poverty,
colonialism, war.

I also have to say that I surprised myself by speaking as a rhino in the first place!

When we read, "It is hard to keep circling around the thing that happened and not say it. But it is also hard to say it. So, I circle some more until it tells itself. I can trust that it will," *I can't help but think of this as a description of this piece's meditative modular structure. Does this passage in some way describe your writing process? (And/or, how do you usually find the structures for your pieces?)*

It does reflect my writing process. My MFA is in poetry, but I write fiction. Or I write really long poems that look like stories.

I saw the poet Alice Oswald read in New York City a few days after Sandy. It was an incredibly raw time. She read from <u>Memorial</u>, which is her translation of the <u>Iliad</u>, except that it contains only the death scenes of the 200 soldiers killed within that story. Well, it contains their death scenes, with alternating blocks of similes. Oswald had memorized her entire reading, which was about thirty minutes long. I felt relieved, but also punched in the gut, when the similes came. They allowed a break from death, but contained such menace, beauty and loss that they didn't relieve much intensity.

I knew that I wanted something like that for "Land Beast". I wanted to form circles of story between present and past; to have her firmly rooted and also in the sea.

I write some linear pieces, but usually I lose interest in them. I structure my pieces in a way that allows memory and trauma to surface in an organic way. I'm most interested in what characters hide from themselves. That interest is best explored out of time.

ABOUT THE AUTHOR

Kate Wyer is the author of the novel *Black Krim*, which was nominated for the Debut-litzer from Late Night Library. Her manuscript, *Girl, Cow*, is a semi-finalist for the Omnidawn Fabulist Fiction Chapbook Contest. Wyer's work can be found in *The Collagist*, *Unsaid*, *PANK*, *Necessary Fiction*, *Exquisite Corpse*, and other journals. She attended the Summer Literary Seminars in Lithuania on a fellowship from *FENCE*. Wyer lives in Baltimore and works in the public mental health system.

ABOUT THE ARTIST

Katie Feild has been living in Bflat7 for years, and is approximately Gflat7 in height (though some days she springs to Fmajor). at times, her hair is ferocious. she treats each project she meets like a person. she loves love, and works and plays like the rest of you. and she'd prefer to hear all about yourself.

ACKNOWLEDGEMENTS

Thank you to Matt Bell for first publishing Land Beast, Part I and II in The Collagist, and for using it on panel discussions about eco-fabulism. I'm incredibly grateful for your support.

Thank you to Katie Feild for her beautiful illustrations and book design. Land Beast reached another level of consciousness with your vision.

Thank you to Clint Wyer, always, for your endless encouragement.

Thank you to everyone who practices compassion towards all beings.

PROCEEDS

100% of the proceeds from the sale of this book are donated to the following charities:

International Rhino Federation
http://www.rhinos.org/

Center for Biological Diversity
http://www.biologicaldiversity.org/

African Wildlife Federation
https://www.awf.org/